In The Midst Of Me

The Journey

Shamina N. Williams

Life Lines Professional Services, LLC

To Vic,
Keep sharing your
light, inspiring and
encouraging us all!!!!

~Shamina

In The Midst of Me Copyright © 2020 by Shamina N. Williams   All rights reserved.
wwww.lifelinesllc.com
@shaminanicole
ISBN: 9780578661650

Cover design by: Tuwana Turner, cincerely@yahoo.com
Printed in the United States of America

This book is dedicated to Dre, who reawakened the writing spirit in me. One day I was sitting in the public library perusing some material and this young man sat in a seat across from me, sharing the same table, we shared a nod hello. A few moments later he asked if he could share something with me and he reached across the table handing me a sheet of paper. I began to read...

"Her face is as legendary as Nefertiti, enlightening me, her soft flesh beams with a shimmering glow, God sculpted her face and made a creation to look upon and marvel over. Indulged by her creamy caramel toffee complexion, her eyes I gaze into.

Hypnotized, mesmerized, and paralyzed, being lost in you was a playground of inspiration. You are a revelation of passionate creation."

I thanked him and told him I used to love writing and we conversed a bit more and shared numbers in hopes that I would make it out to an open mic event. That was over 13 years ago. Dre, thank you for giving me hope, a bigger sense of pride and the will to pursue a career in writing. This book is also dedicated to Deiara and Haiden whom give me the strength to go on living every day. Mommy loves you! Know that I am on my path....and a special thanks to Cjay who typed up the first manuscript of this book when it was titled "Do You Feel Me," thank s for your hands and support. I would also like to give a HUGE, BIG thank you to my friend, writing partner, biggest supporter La (Lonique), I don't think I would have arrived here without you, thank you. And much love and thanks to family and friends who stuck by me and didn't give up on me while I was writing this book. To my Father, who has kept me and I know He's still working on me, I give Him all the praise.

Contents

Foreword

In The Midst of Me... Sometimes in life, the hardest thing to do is to look deep within ourselves to find the answers to some of life's dilemmas. It can expose a great sense of vulnerability when we decide to peel away each layer of ourselves and delve into the good, the bad, and the ugly of our own existence. Although, all these things combined with each of our life experiences creates the person that we have grown to be, it's still a difficult task to encounter. In doing so, it's almost inevitable that we uncover some of the deepest pains, the happiest joys, the biggest regrets, the greatest accomplishments, the worst fears, the best attributes, and the many flaws that embody us as a person. There's a wide range of emotion that will accompany these things that will surely leave questions in our minds as we contemplate the decisions we've made and the roads we've traveled. Granted, this process is tough on us emotionally, but at the end of the process, it can prove to be an exhilarating experience that frees us of the baggage that we tend to hold on to. Now imagine if you decided to document all these emotions, fears, joys, regrets, mishaps, accomplishments and publish them for the world to read...The vulnerability that you felt will now be multiplied by a thousand as you invite everyone into your inner world. Would the reader of these inner thoughts judge you? Laugh at you? Feel sorry for you? Cry with you? Maybe, but what about the people who may be going through the exact same emotions and thinking that no one can relate to the pain they are experiencing.

That alone may give them the will to keep pushing through the obstacles that life has placed in their paths. The funny thing about emotions is that we all have them. Some of us disguise them a little better than others, but in each of us they exist. That's what makes us human. The ability to share these emotions is a gift that not many of us possess. Those that are not blessed with this gift may never feel the relief that accompanies the purging and release of letting go of the baggage of past life's experiences. The toughest person that we will ever face and answer to is the one in the mirror. But once we find those answers, there may be millions of people that can learn from those experiences. As in any book, you have to complete and close one chapter before you can open and enjoy the next one. So with that being said, I ask...when your book of life ends, will there be many open ended unfinished chapters or will it flow like a great novel of experiences and journeys that were uncovered when you looked "In the Midst of Me"?

Written by Lonique Burnett

Introduction

These poems are intended to expose your thinking to issues that may have never crossed your mind and to also help you feel what's on my mind. These poems convey a few different themes. Some of anger, love, relationships, temptation, innocence, morality and most of all, compassion. As you read, I hope the words evoke immediate sensation within you. I love all my brothers and sisters out there who are on their grind, existing, and just wanted to let you know I feel you, all the emotions, struggles, and fears we all experience. I decided to break this book down into four sections. The first one being Faith, the second, Children and Society, third, Inappropriate Thoughts and Behavior (with a little foul language and humor) and lastly, Love and Life. We all have our personal struggles and we also have a struggle as a people. I do not want that to be forgotten, especially with the younger generation, which is why I come to you with my thoughts and my innermost feelings and desires. I also want people to know that you have to be honest about your past in order to be successful in your future. So...take your time and enjoy life, keep God in your heart because without Him, you will have no peace. Be sure to chase your dreams and not the mighty dollar and all things will fall in place as they should. Don't be alarmed, nor attempt to judge me because of some of the language used in this work as I am In The Midst of Me, loving, learning, failing, growing, building and succeeding...PEACE and Blessings!

1-Faith
Standing Still
Fully Aware
Meet and Greet
Exhaustion
Where The Hell Am I?
Anointing
The Scarf
Untitled
A Letter to God
Living
He Walks With Me
What Do I Do?

2-Children and Society
Come Here
The Mode
I wish They Were All My Babies
I am Cool
My Child
The Beauty in You
Sssh

3-Inappropriate Thoughts and Behavior
It Finally Came
He Said, She Said
Someone Elses's
Demoiselle
Questions
Is it The heart or Hurt
Numb
Damn
Remembering Old and Young Times

1

FAITH

"Now faith is the substance of things hoped for, the evidence of things not yet seen...Hebrews 11:1 (NKJV)"

To go through life, you must have faith, even if you are not the most spiritual person. We all, at some point or another, hope, wish, want for so many things, some of which we strive to make happen, other times, we just think things will magically appear. But it is our faith that thrusts us forward in all situations, knowing, trusting that all things will work in our favor.

Standing Still

Everything is passing me by
The excitement of spring, which I love so dearly
The eventfulness of the summer and its sun, which I bask in
The winds of fall leaning into winter.
It's been passing me by for the past two years and I fear that it will go on forever
You know...standing still. Me standing still....
I love the summer blue skies and the beautiful butterflies,
The fall and winter midnight blue skies, some nights so clear you can see the ocean.
But it's morning before I can sit on my porch and revel in these

sites
The winter winds, brisk and cold,
Fresh air I want to stand and breathe it all in to see if any snow is coming.
But I can't. I am standing still.
While all of life and its wonders are passing me by.
While time is ticking and Monday becomes Sunday after Sunday becomes Monday for me
because ...I am standing still.
I can't stand still too much longer, because something or some-one is going to knock me down...
If I am still standing still.

Fully Aware

I am fully aware of the state I'm currently in
I am fully aware of the skin I'm in
I am fully aware of my financial status
I am fully aware that I am a mom and my name ain't Gladys
I am fully aware of what it means to be desperate
I am fully aware that I'm not married
I am fully aware that loneliness is a state of mind
I am fully aware that I can do better
I am fully aware that I need some help
I am fully aware that I can't give up
I am fully aware that a day comes and goes
I am fully aware that you shouldn't waste time on yesterday's woes
I am fully aware that I can do anything
I am fully aware that I can create a plan and follow it
I am fully aware that my eyes and ears need to be open and my mouth needs to be shut
I am fully aware of all the feelings in my gut
I am fully aware that I will overcome, conquer and love will take over and run my mind

Meet and Greet

You never know what God has in store for you.
New friends, new acquaintances, new relationships to be

formed.

We're at a meet and greet, and all of our spirits seem to be at peace, in a different place, different space, different secrets to keep.

Brought together by chance, our femininity intertwined in a dance of fellowship, laughter and stories of true blue survival.

All shapes, all sizes, all prizes in our own right! The meet and greet...we're not here all soft and sweet. We're here, open, honest and sharing our defeats, our conquest, our war scars.

The meet and greet. I had some reservations; some hesitations because I didn't know who I was gonna meet.

All queens, Black beauties in our glory, sittin back, chillin, sharing our stories...knowledge...making things solid. The meet and greet!!!

This piece was inspired by a friend who held a gathering so that all of her mutual friends could meet each other. We had to share something about ourselves and I stated I was a poet. Needless to say there was a woman who challenged me, told me I had to write something before the night ended...and Meet and Greet was created. Thanks for the inspiration that night Kelly!

Exhaustion
I am so tired of being sick and tired
When will I ever be tired of being sick and tired

You know...I never thought this was how my young life would be, struggling at age 28 since 23

I'm tired of begging niggas for money, but can't help but say "show me the damn money"

I never knew or understood how people could work just to be broke, but now I understand

I want for so much, and its not even the material possessions, money cant buy you love, happiness, nor a piece of mind, but it can help you through the tough times, clothing for your children and putting food on the table, not to mention incentive for doing great in school, and helping with chores around the house, oh and you can't forget basketball, tap and soccer, hell, before and after school care because I am a single parent with little physical support

I am simply tired of being sick and tired

I wish it were easy just to change your mind about the way you live and treat certain situations differently, but I guess its just easier sometimes to wallow in self pity than it is to stress about everything

I am so tired of being sick and tired, and today I will fight to make a change for the better

Today I will tap into my inner self, into God who lives in me and I will begin to live through Him

With no stress and no doubt, I know that things will all work themselves out.

Where The Hell Am I?
It is so dark and cold out here. I am not afraid of anything or anyone because I have no fear of anyone or anything...But I wish someone could tell me where the hell I am?

I am a woman blessed with the spirit of God, but yet I am lost in a world, which sometimes it seems, there is no God?

Where the hell am I?...I am beside the man with all the riches in the world, all the kindness of his heart and all the shallowness of a mark ass nigga?

Am I with that woman with no direction no ambition no happiness in her life...am I that woman?

Am I that woman on the corner with a ten dollar shirt two dollar skirt and a five cent pair of shoes?...No... I don't think I've ever been there, but maybe pretty damn close!

I am in a state of confusion! That's where the hell I am!

Why the hell am I sitting in this meeting with these people with different backgrounds, different levels of education, but I am sitting here with them with no feeling or sensation to continue on with this stuff, this bullshit, this sooo unfulfilling shit!

I am riding with this man, my friend, who is facing ten years for some dumb shit. I think about his children, his mother, brothas, his father, his sistas...What will be of his future because of his past? Where the hell is the compassion for our young Black males?

Where the hell am I? Where the hell are we as a community, a family, a church, and a world?

Where the hell am I?
Somebody answer me please!!!!

Oooh...let me close my eyes...breathe deep...

I am sitting in my study with the kids out back, my water wall is running, my ceiling is that of the sky between sunset and sunrise, my wall is textured of that huge wave I always envision on that ship floating across the Atlantic...I lay across my chaise with pen in one hand and pad on my lap... I'm sitting listening to Stevie and I am so in tact.

That's where I am...that's exactly where I am...

It's really funny to me when I ponder some of these pieces. This poem was given as a challenge to me. My friend told me to write something based around the title...I think when I am put on the spot, some of my innermost thoughts are put on paper. Written for you Trey.

Anointing
You cannot tell me anything about who I am in Christ. It goes in one ear and out the other.
You try your best to get me to speak of my situations, but I am always in meditation.
You cannot tempt me; you can try all you want. I don't fear you or anything you're talkin bout.
I am a joint heir with Christ! He said, put on his whole armor, so

for that I have no strife.

I once was ruled by flesh, and I let him creep in and out...until I walked in a new light that illuminated from Him, from within. At one time I was too immature to see it. I use to pull my hair.... but now, I just trust with all thine heart and flow in His anointing.

The Scarf

This time she has that scarf on her head, and guess what? Now there's no tread
She's gorgeous but baldhead, no make-up at all...

She has that scarf on her head, and guess what? She rocks a few wigs, one I really like, and it doesn't take away from her might that she has wound up so tight

She has that scarf on her head, but guess what? It does nothing for her arthritic hands and toes that chemo is turning into goblin molds

The tint is changing and poor thing, she doesn't even want me to massage those toes, the toes I always caress and console

Oh yeah, she's stronger than five generations, oh I wish I could be as strong as that woman with the scarf on her head

And guess what? That's my mom, that's right...it's what I said

Cancer, we got you beat. You can have her appetite and some of her weight, but cancer, the lady with the scarf on her head, she has you beat!

Thank God for chemo and the blood of His son, cause she has that scarf on her head, but she's shinning bright full of life

That's my mom, Connie's her name, my mom with the scarf on her head.

This poem was actually written after a poem titled Tears in an upcoming section. Both The Scarf and Tears were inspired by my mother's bouts with breast cancer, she is a two time survivor.

UNTITLED

I so wish that things were ever so still.

Like if one day could be dragged into two.

If I could be as still as the times and cherish each

minute of my day as if it were an hour.

I would sit and breathe easy, clean all the cobwebs in the corner,

and clear all dust bunnies from the floor.

Clean out that cluttered closet and even more. Throw out those

notes from freshman year, and begin to clean all my fears.

Take a bath with some relaxing salts,

sip a glass of wine and listen to matters of the heart.

Get still and quiet and evaluate my life, let

go of 10 years of stress and strife.

Wake early and study, and run my mile,

Have breakfast with my daughter and enjoy her smile.

A Letter to God

You tell me to come to you, but I'm frustrated, I'm angry and not exactly sure at this very moment, how to come to you.

I'm not angry or frustrated with you, just wondering how I keep ending up here.

I swear, I really just want a glass of red wine, some purp, and some time alone, just enough to take the edge off. I've been wanting to cry all day, actually since last night, but not sure what I'm wanting to cry for.

You see God, I can't win for losing, seems like the more I see the light at the end of the tunnel, the darker and more strange my path becomes.

I'm tired Lord, tired of running, tired of not making enough money, simply tired of being what others need and want me to be at this very moment. I know I need to show you I am a good steward over what I have, but, come on, what I have just ain't getting it done...But still Jesus, I'm thankful because I'm standing upright, I have my whole mind, my limbs are in tact, I am breathing and writing and I have my sight.

I am feeling so overwhelmed with it all, new expectations, new demands, new baby, many different circumstances. I don't wanna talk, I simply wanna get away, runaway...just for a lil while. And when I get back, bills will be paid, house will be clean, dogs will be bathed and the kids will both behave.

We have all been in a place, no matter how well we know God, how saved and spiritual we are, we have been in that place where it seems our prayers are not being answered, or not being answered fast enough. So, I wrote this letter to God, and shortly after, my circumstances changed. He brings us through our tests and trials so that we will have a testimony that can only be explained by, The Hand of God (SMILING).

Living

You know what, I don't need you. I never have. So why do you steadily approach me only wondering what I have. I can move on and through any situation and never look back. I packed my bags and left your stack buried under trash, way in the back.

I am happy, fueled by the spirit. It shows in my walk, shines through my teeth and is seen in my stance. I don't proclaim it ...it simply shines through.
So why are you so concerned with my relationship with God, my finances, my relationship with you?

Live your life cuz, cause I'm definitely living mine!!!

I get to see my daughter's big bright smiles and I am more intrigued by their conversation versus those of my peers. She brushes my hair and showers me with hugs; she also loves to give gifts of rocks, flowers and shrubs. She loves the dog, but hates when he licks her face, I'm living through her as well, and it's simply because of grace.

My family, through good and bad, withstands because of the love that binds. We don't worry or fret or wallow on the ground.

We live our lives cuz, and you need to live yours.

I'm not in debt up to my neck, and I'm not driving a 2020 BMW. I don't owe on students loans,...and yes....I know myself and my joint heirs are all sitting on thrones.

Live your life cuz, cause I'm definitely living mine!

He Walks With Me

I know He walks with me...has been with me since my conception...here for all eternity

The devil knows this, which is why he tries to trick me, get me to believe some of my insanity

I know he only comes to steal, kill and destroy, but my Father has shown me what He has in store for me

My world has become the thoughts inside my head, which I have not fully protected and the devil has tried to come and infect it with lies and sins from my past

I know He walks with me, His grace and mercy are evident with every picture I see, every moment that He has kept and saved me

There are times when my soul cries and He has been the only to console me

My days will be spent in prosperity and my years in pleasure, as long as I obey and serve Him

I know He walks with me, although there may be times I forget, I know He never has

The blessings on my life, so many I can't count...I know I can be obedient to His word, and I know what my life is like when I doubt

He shows His face to me continuously, even during the times when I didn't want to see

I know He walks with me and will continuously keep me, no matter the space I sometimes find myself

He walks with me

What Do I Do
I keep asking myself why am I still here, why do I leave him and still I go back

I know there is so much missing, lacking, but yet I act as if everything is in tact

I am falling apart daily on the inside and I try not to talk to God too much cause He told me to go a long time ago

I don't understand it, the thoughts that consume me daily, I'm probably borderline insane, dealing with this married man and all his different names

I find myself holding on, clinging to his promises instead of the promises of God

No wonder I feel like sometimes I should just hide on the inside

I know this isn't living and that I am closing myself up from so much, for real,

I ask myself, who are you this time, this day...what can I say

I am desperately trying to seek out what God has destined for me, but I am lost inside the wrong cup of tea

I am steadily losing myself and God's promises to be

I cant express myself to him, although I've tried at times, other times I think, why bother if you still allow yourself to be treated in such a way

The blame is all my own, the responsibility, respect and courage is what I should own,

But at times I feel I will be alone, and he does love me, but not whole

I need to live my life openly and free of the lies, the little secrets, free of living alone

I realize I will never be ok in this situation, but still, I endure like there are no other fish in the ocean

What do you do when you feel the one you love isn't the one God
fashioned for you
What will I do, when will I do, how will I do, to completely move
on and get over you

*There's a lot of hurt, pain and confusion in this piece. I by no means
condone adultery, and we as adults make choices that we have to live
with. Ultimately, the discretion was revealed, I should have been
woman enough to walk away, but I didn't have the courage to do so, I
loved him and was in love with him, but learned some very valuable
lessons when I finally did. I learned to value myself as a woman,
I recognized my worth, and rebuilt my self-esteem, because some-
where I thought this was what I deserved, and clearly, it was not. I
truly understand what it means to walk by faith and not by sight.
What we see, coupled with our emotions can get us in some really
bad situations. So now, I learn to go to God with everything, my
anger, my wants and needs, and I go to Him with gratitude because
I know He is doing something that I can't see or imagine. My faith
in God is all I have and that's why faith was the first section of this
work.*

2

C hildren and Society

"The test of the morality of a society is what it does for its children." Dietrich Bonhoeffer - German Protestant theologian & anti-Nazi activist (1906 - 1945)

This section involves some of my most intimate feelings regarding things I've experienced and never shared. It also involves my feelings towards the state of today's youth and society as a whole. My hopes are that this section intrigues you and provokes thought...leading to some sort of action within your very own community.

Come Here
Come here
Tell me your problems
I'll listen
With my ears
You can bring me your heart
I'll protect it
Nourish it
Keep it close to me and I won't let it break

Come here
Bring me your tongue
You don't have to say a word
I will hold your hands
And I will listen to your eyes

If you want, you can give me them too
I'll face the world for you

Hold up your hands and lift up your head and breathe in all the
love that is here for you
If you can't
I'll tell you, but not with my mouth, but with my heart

Come here...please, come here with love
Come here, with your mind and I will give you my soul

The Mode

life is what you make it
that's what we've been told
but how can you go about making it if you're a lost soul

there are no fathers and the mothers are not as bold
as they have been sold into "I don't give a shit" mode

life is what you make it
it's what I was told
but I was raised with both parents and excellence is what I was
sold
raised by aunts and uncles, not simply the two
that's one of the pieces lacking in today's "I don't give a shit"
mode

our culture is so self centered
no one wants to lend a helping hand
to help guide the lives of so many misguided youths

life is what you make it
its absolutely true
if you want to be a thug, a nuisance or even a disrespecting fool
you'll find your life wasted with no tools used
prison will be your home and that sub-culture is one of doom

take advantage of all opportunities
leave no stone unturned, this world is yours
so think smart, reach out, give back
you will end up sitting on a pot of gold

I Wish They Were All My Babies

Look at all those babies, being raised and not raised by babies.
Two pulling at her legs and one is in her belly and I don't see a daddy anywhere around
Lil boy with a gold nugget in his ear and braids going all through his head, lil wife beater and shit.

I don't understand this entire cycle we're in. As a people, what do we do? I didn't boo Bill Cosby, what about you?

Pants sagging off their asses, and all this junk hanging round their neck and they have the audacity to walk cross my block smoking a blunt. Go in front of your house and do that mess!

Yeah, I yelled at them, but then I became fearful, thought to myself, these young boys could be packin.

Lil grown ass girls, thinking they know more than me. I try to talk to em you know. I see them outside. Shirt too tight, skirt way too short. Hell, her breast are bigger than mine. Lil sis, be careful, what they don't see they surely can't miss, and he most definitely wouldn't have you out here trying to resist him. You're putting it all out there for him is what he's thinking. You're my young sisters. I'm trying to help you become aware, baby, that this life ain't gravy. Respect yourself sisters.

But, they have their noses up in the air at me. They don't care what I'm trying to say, because their momma's are probably the same way, doin the same thing.

I would like to gather all my young brothers and sisters to let them know that the images they consistently see are not really those of you and me. Come see me every Wednesday and I will show you and tell you what it really means to be young, Black, fly and free. I will liberate your mind and show you a world of non-conformity.

I was a baby you see, a lil young sister myself, still in some ways that I can see. Plus I have a baby who watches me, and I'm not married you see.

Come my babies and learn with me. Know that you are bright, intelligent and the leaders of our upcoming generation, and with your ambition and skills directed in the right way, you can become more than anyone ever thought you could be and you will realize that death and prison are not options you see!

Come my babies and learn with me.

I Am Cool

I am cool in this skin. People move me and walk by me, walk with me and then avoid me
when I say I am HIV positive.

I am cool in this skin, body changing, but I am on this cocktail that makes my days bearable, livable, free of most pain.

I am cool in this skin. I can't be angry, not take responsibility for my actions, nor spread this unforgiving disease with no conscious, as some people do.

I am cool in this skin, always thought I would be, until I was told I contracted HIV. I am heterosexual and thought I was being safe with my partner of 11 years who I never once thought was bisexual, a drug addict or simply involved in unsafe sexual practices. Black, White, Hispanic, male, female, working class, middle class, upper class.

I am cool in this skin as long as I use protection. And you will remain cool in your skin if you take charge and become proactive about your lifestyle and sexual behavior.
Stay cool in your skin and wrap it up!!!
Dedicated to all my brothers and sisters who are infected. And to those of you who haven't, GET TESTED!!!

MY CHILD

You were only 3 ½ months old

You were kicking and growing, creating your soul

You had eyes, fingers, and a nose, but who knows

If it was mine, your dads, or your own.

I never touched your little feet

or even felt your heart beat.

I remember the day you were killed but

not the day you were never born.

You would have been born in July

but I was too stupid to let that time go by.

Forgive me for what I have done, but

I was young and it was more my mothers decision than mine.

But that's no excuse

I miss you my child, and I just ask you to forgive me.

It's important to practice safe sex for a plethora of reasons. Disease, unwanted pregnancies, relational and emotional problems, these all stem from unhealthy sexual practices. I am not against abortion, but it is not a form of birth control, and it seems that more women use it as so, so please, practice safe sex and teach your children about healthy and safe sexual practices.

The Beauty in You
how unexpected they were
me so young, so inexperienced

but
He blessed me with them
chose me to carry them in my womb
the unspeakable joy, pain, sorrow, disappointment, fear, all occupied the same space

physical and emotional wounds
loneliness, bitterness
but
your first kick over shadowed all of that
the beauty in you I couldn't see
I could only imagine what might be
children, all mine to raise and introduce the world to, not you to the world

nights of fright, fear
how was I going to do this
feelings of despair
but
He equipped me
Didn't matter what my bank account said, didn't matter what my mother, father nor brother said
He knew it was well, and He knew His fortitude in me

the beauty in you
how good it was when I played music to you and watched my belly dance
or
when I rocked in the chair and read a story to you allowing my nerves to calm
watching you on the sonogram, covering your face with your little big hands
turning your face to us as if to ask, what are ya'll doin out there?

God has been so good, so good
I know that I must do better, and He knows I will do better
the beauty is knowing the blessing to me, to be your mother
even though I thought it was before my time
He knew the beauty manifested in you would help me to recog-

nize the beauty in me
the beauty in you helped raise me so that you can be the best you,
you can be
I'm far from perfect
I don't use it as an excuse
but
it is definitely a reflection of me in you and Him in me
thank God, thank God for the beauty in you
with love and tenderness Deiara and Haiden,
Your mom.

Sssh...
Sssh

Hey there, you're so pretty! Oh just look at that smile and those

pretty teeth. Ssh, I won't hurt you. I'm your uncle, your brother,

your daddy, your principal, your teacher, I won't hurt you.

Hey there, give me a hug, ooh you feel so

soft. Oh, you're so pretty...

Can I kiss your hand?

"yeah...?"

Ooh, can I kiss your cheek, I won't hurt you. I'm going

to kiss you on that beautiful smile...is that ok?

"um...no, I don't think so!"

I'm not going to hurt you...

Oh, your lips are so sweet. I'm going to feel you

here, oh, and there, ooh, and there.

I'm going to kiss you between your legs

and it's going to feel so good...

32

"oh, no, I can't"

Sure you can, I'm not going to hurt you...

"oh, it feels good but there is something wrong..."

Oh no darling, you are fine....now it's my time to

feel good. Let me show you what else you can

do with that beautiful smile of yours...

"oh no, I've never seen a penis before...!"

It's ok darling, it won't bite you, besides, I'm your

uncle, your brother, your daddy, your principal,

your teacher, I won't hurt you.

How about close your eyes and pretend you're sucking

on an ice cream cone and then pretend your sucking

on a lollipop....ooh darling, that feels so good...

"I can't..."

Ssh, yes you can darling...it feels so good. Now lay

down, I have something else to show you...

"no, I'm only a child..."

It's ok...I will not hurt you!

"yes, it hurts really bad...please, oh please stop!!!"

But he didn't. Embarrassed and ashamed, not

knowing she had done nothing wrong, she throws

her bloody panties away and never tells a soul.

At an early age, bout 8 or 9, I experienced sexual abuse and didn't

33

reveal it until I was an adult. For some reason, I thought I was to blame and that I did something wrong, not realizing I was a child and innocent. After these first experiences, I was later a victim of acquaintance rape in middle school and high school. Sexual abuse is still an issue that is swept under the rug in our society and we must educate our children about these acts, and let them know its ok to come forward and tell someone about it and dispel the stigmas associated with it. We also need to teach our children that no means no, regardless of the situation and to teach our children how to avoid certain situations as best as possible.

3

I nappropriate Thoughts and Behavior (with a little foul language and humor)

"I just can't be all easy, just satisfying and pleasing" – Jill Scott (Making You Wait)

It Finally Came
where have you been
I've been looking for you for quite some time
you had me thinking of baby blue and pretty in pink
little bonnets and even baby minks

my back and legs are aching and I am seeing some spots
you had me wondering if this was my right clock or should I
make a trip to the clips cause my clock gots to be telling the
wrong time...
or was it God's sign?

oh...thank you
now I finally see some flow
It finally came!
I will put that snake in his bag and make sure I eat my little pink
cake

He Said, She Said
He said he wanted to smell it

I said put your face in it
He said he wanted to taste it
I said he would need to suck it
He said he wanted to kiss it
I said I want you to lick it
He said he wanted to put his finger in it
I said sure but hum on it
He said he wanted to squeeze on it
I said nibble on it
He said he wanted to blow on it
I said put sum ice on it, chew sum mint gum and nibble on it
He said he wanted to watch
I said why not
He said he wanted to tease
I said I wanna be pleased
He said he wanted to grab an pull
I said I wanted more and more
He said he wanted to hit the floor
I said I couldn't take no more
He said, She said and they went they separate ways and slept in their respective beds

It's really tough to be single and live holy. We get caught up so quickly, especially women, with our emotions and a charismatic spirit, and before we know it, we've been talked out of our drawls by someone we barely took the time to get to know. Ladies, hold on to your cookies, as long as you see fit. You can date and live holy without having sex, believe me, it's all in the decisions we make and exploring other methods of intimacy and knowing that there are sevral different types of intimacy. Get to know yourselves and explore these. But sex is also fine to, whatever is right for you.

Someone Else's
He's not home with me...
You see...
He's with his wife and family...what a joy to be with a wife and 6 lil feet.

He's not home with me…
You see…
He just left me…to go home to be with his wife and little three.

He's not home with me…
You see…
I made a meal fit for a king…and he ate…and then ate me…and he still went home to his wife and their little three.

He's not home with me…
But, you see…
I am home with me.

Demoiselle

I am not your fuck toy.
I am not your mistress.
I am not your phat thighs, long legged booby.
I am not the love of your life; I am not your WIFE!
I am not your beck and call girl; I am not
your high heels with a thong girl.
I am not your wettest pussy girl,
Deepest pussy girl,
Pretty smelling pussy girl,
Your pussy taste good girl.
I am not the; What you need girl?
Take this one thousand dollars and pay some of your bills girl.
I am not your living secrets keep this quiet girl.
I am not your wait on me girl.
Your, take out of town trick girl.
I am not the; I love how you smell, suck, and fuck girl, but
you can't be my girl, girl, but my girl on the side girl.
I am not the girl that becomes complacent or comfortable.
I am not the girl with no desires.
I am not the girl who depends on another.
I am not the girl who enjoys living in secret.
I am not the girl who will act as if some of this shit don't exist.

I am not the girl you will manipulate.
I am not the girl you will take advantage of, the girl you think
you can change my views and opinions to fit your own girl.
I am not the girl who will get high all her life
and let life and time pass her by.
I am not the girl who thinks wealth and
riches is what life is all about.
I am definitely not a girl!

This piece above was written during hurt and anger...and it was written over 15 years ago. Interesting to reflect and to see how much I've grown, recognizing when I became a, woman.

Questions...

I'm scared to death to commit and I ain't afraid to admit it. You had me, hook, line and sinker...and then you raised issues of trust wit your response to a pussy pic in your phone that wasn't mine you see. Yeah, you put a ring on it...came in playing supa man like you could handle it...me with a 12 year old and an infant that was 2 and a half months old. I asked you never to hurt me, never to lie to me...and I trusted you with a part of me that I didn't know existed. You found me...but then you had me and it feels in a matter of months you took me for granted. Fuck my needs, my wants, my desires...fuck that man I was smitten by, fell in love with...now I just wanna say bye bye...I let you go, you came back. Stating you wanted to take another crack at it, but here we are and I am still asking myself can I accept you for who you are, are my days better, enhanced with or without you. You see, I have a lot of maturing to do, and I am not mature enough to meet your needs if your saying fuck mine, but I need mine met to. Counseling is not a fix all, but hell, when we leave, our perceptions of the experience are totally different and we are not coming away from it on the same page. But yet, you want to try and force me to take those vows, say I do, I will, but right now I can't, I won't, I'm not sure how with you. My frustrations are turning into resentments, my needs falling on deaf ears...if it's been like this in less than two years...how will I feel in five, 10, 15 years from now. I don't know what to do...do I accept and push through...learn to be the bigger person...is this something I can do...

Is It The Heart or Hurt?

We were special friends before we were lovers.
We were there for each other before we became
intimate with one another
Yeah it's true, you are still here, but I am
slowly, but surely fading.
You tell me I'm cruel, hateful, and mean when I
want to be, but I know when I am this way
You say cold harsh things, but you never recognize it
You are cruel with your words
Devilish with your eyes
Innocent with your smile
Intoxicating with your kiss
Dangerous with your LOVE
Gentle (at times) with your touch
We made a mistake
I made a huge mistake
I thought...
I could handle the more than special friends
I thought I could handle your not being able to love anyone
I thought I could handle your attitude that
you are unconscious of at all times
I thought I could be patient
I thought I could marry you
I thought I could love you
Even more than what I do
I CAN'T
It hurts too much
ITS OVER, IT'S GONE
Everything is gone
I can no longer wait
Patience is not a virtue that I possess

ITS OVER!
You will never marry!
You will never love!
You will never get close enough to anyone
to really ever feel anything

NUMB

Did I love you? Do you love me? Do you still love me? Do I still have feelings for you? Do you miss me? Do I miss you? How can I ever know?

I was numb when I was with you. I put my feelings on hold when

I was with you because I could no longer feel you, because I had

been hurt by you and you disregarded everything I said. So in

reality I can see I didn't make myself numb. **YOU** made me numb.

So I can't answer your questions. **YOU** answer them for yourself.

Because numb I am and numb I will always be when it comes to

YOU.

Today, I could never tell another person how they feel or what they will ever feel. And of course, we are never emotionally numb, right. We suppress and as a woman today, I can only love myself, know and be confident in who I am and don't settle for anything that does not give me the type of love I need and deserve. Smiling for Matthew (Matchew).

Damn

Damn...Damn...Damn...

here it goes...I've been tryna to behave, trying not to let my pussy go insane
but boy is he pretty, yes indeed, boy is he pretty...milk chocolate that can melt in my mouth and my hand
but damn, I must resist and withstand.

he held and squeezed my hand and it was almost orgasmic...

he then caressed my face, legs and calves and shit...damn I'm bout ready to bust...but I must resist and withstand.

his lips are as soft as mine

I'm in a daze, almost swept away in a haze of passion and pure delight.
this man's arms are as big as my thighs and I can tell he truly wants to get inside, and I can tell, if he gets the chance, he's going to try to eat me alive.

damn, I close my eyes and I smell his issey miyake scent as his lips caress the peak of my mounds, oh my gosh, I moan and sigh... Please, Please, Please stop...

but oh how I would like to continue, put my mouth on em, as he is standing at ease now, I suck, I lick, damn, not this quick. I catch myself, I stop...damn, if it happens I know it's gonna be the shit.

damn, slow down, come back down...

he whispers in my ear...I block out his words, intoxicated, again, there goes his issey miyake scent...
he grabs the back of my neck, damn I wanna feel his thrusts and thrust it right back...legs wide open and peeled back...

Damn...Damn...Damn...not yet!

Remembering Old and Young Times in The City (Chester, PA)
I remember back in the day I had the purple and white high
top Reeboks with triple slouch socks of different colors
I remember back in the day I had my first
pair of cloth hot pink K-Swiss.
Remember back in the day double dutch and paybacks?
I remember back in the day the block parties in the Bennett
Homes, the block parties on 8th street, and I will never forget
the ones where I would dance until I dropped to 2 Live Crew's
"DooDoo Brown", and "Come Test the Rocket Launcher"
I also remember the parties at the Fair Ground Center,
that I was never able to attend, but would always
sneak out to, just to get in trouble back then

I remember back in the day sneaking out of the house
wit your girlfriend who spent the night so you could go
ride in cars with boys who really lived the wrong life.
Remember the initial rings, bamboo earrings,
gold ropes and herringbone chains?
Remember those fights between the Eastside
and the William Penn?
I remember those fights you had with
those silly ass upperclassmen
I remember freshman year at Chester High during
football camp and band camp playing with some
of the players near the locker rooms
I remember when I dropped my books between classes on the
fourth floor C side and left them out of embarrassment
I remember those times when you used to hitchhike
Remember those Nova's, Audi's, and the UMBRO gear?
I remember sitting on the corner of 8th and Barclay when
we would burn on one another, have water fights, snowball
fights, and hell, we did survive a drive by or two.
Remember when you were president of the Itty Bitty Titty
Committee, and you flashed the boys one day who gave you that
title just to show them they weren't so Itty Bitty after all?
I remember going to the stinking boys club, or how bout
the YWCA in the summer when we would swim for
hours just for a dollar before they shut it down.
Remember back in the day Thanksgiving Day football
games at the A-Field where you would stand
wit ya crew or sit wit ya girls?
How about the Christmas basketball games at Chester High?
And you knew someone would be fighting afterwards or well,

hell, shooting afterwards while you're trying to get home
I remember my old and young times
I remember Sunday dinner after church, collard
greens with smoked ham hocks, macaroni and
cheese, cornbread and fried chicken
I remember corn pudding, my momma's peach cobbler,
and my mom-moms 7 Up pound cake
I remember playing in the field of the Bennett Homes. Getting
chicken pox and missing my first visit to Disney World
I remember that first boy I kissed, the first boy I fell in love with.
Remembering old and young times

4

L ove and Life

"See Daddy, sinners have souls too"
– Shug Avery (The Color Purple)

Rejoice

Yes, I must say, I think I've found the one. Yup, the one God has chosen and fashioned just for me. I know it seems a bit crazy, I totally agree...I get it; you may have heard a similar tale from me. But this, this time, it s completely unexplainable, he's resting and residing in a place, space in me that only God has been. Yes. Yes, yes, I knooow, slow your roll, take your time, enjoy it, get to know him, and in time, you'll know.

But I do know. There is no comparison to any other. I'm sure there is so much more to learn, so much more to know, so much more neither of us has told. But I'm thinking we'll be ok and weather any storm. I am complete and whole without him, but I know God will give you the desires of your heart, and my heart was simply waiting, not knowing if it would truly ever experience this part. God knows my heart, surely God has known my heart.

Yes, it's a dream come true, too good to be true. Me falling after one week, that wow, I think I'm in love with you. But hey, what can I say, the feeling is mutual, that's what really brightens my day. Here are smiles inside and out, smileds dancing all around my heart.

Yes, this is the day the Lord has made and I will rejoice and be glad in it.

One day has felt like so many, seven days has felt like a new beginning, many more. I'm thinking the joy of a lifetime with thoughts, dreams, ideas all intertwined.

Yes, I've been bit by the love bug, cupid has hit me with love potion number nine, singing a melody that is simply undefined.

This man has vision, as do I, and we will not perish, but fly and multiply, one with another in perfect peace, knowing that God is our head and the devil is under our feet.

Yes, this is the day the Lord has made and I will rejoice and be glad in it.

Remembrance

I heard your voice last year this time...laughing, wishing well to do's...and it was then I truly recognized something was wrong... that something was going on with you. If I could have gotten there that day I would have, and gave you the biggest embrace I had to give. I wonder what I would have done differently if I would have known it was gonna be the last time I would have the opportunity to talk with you...

Your smile, your love, your friendship brought a peace to my soul always. I miss you Sherene...You were my Reney and I was your Meany...So many memories, none I will forget. I will cherish each and every moment we shared and spent. Cause you were my sister, my strength, and my pride. Only God may know why, still I get by... Who would've known that you would have to go so suddenly, so fast. How could it be, but a sweet memory would be all that we have left, B-E-A-U-T-I-F-U-L gal.

I lost my dear friend during the spring of 2009 when I was expecting my second child. Her death was completely unexpected, and today I still mourn her passing. I met Sherene my freshman year of college and we became friends instantly. I also lost my maternal grandmother weeks before my youngest was born. I have not been able to express her death in words today, but she is lovingly missed.

45

My Forbidden Fruit

You are of such peculiar taste
Yet, not so different,
but different in your own little way

You have the look of that sweet and dark fig tree
and the smell of a chew stick I got off South Street

You are so clean and so appealing; I could just eat you up
and   totally bask in the feeling
Yet...
You are tarnished...bruised more than I would like to
admit
You became a bit spoiled from lying with that bad bunch,
not so bad
But..
that half eaten, half touched, half tasted bunch....but I
truly
love you
of peculiar taste, but I hate to admit...
with you...I will yield and haste,
but I wouldn't if you hadn't already gone to waste
My forbidden fruit.

TEARS

I got that lump in my throat
and my jaws are tight.
I will not let them roll down my cheeks
They are in the back of my eyes
just as wet as they want to be
My hands are sweaty and clammy, and I can hardly swallow
Why are they here?
While I'm just lying in my bed,
I am not lonely or sad
I am loved,
but awaiting my true love.
No, No, No,

I will not let them roll down my face, not today anyway

     I see that couple riding beside me on the road
We are at a stoplight,
and I see man, woman, and child in the back in a car seat
He looks so peaceful and sweet in the back...but...woman is in a
tearful rage while man looks as if he is totally on a different page
     Reminds me soooo much of my stress filled days, but
nope, I will not let them roll down my face,
not today anyway

Do you see that 14-year-old girl pushing that stroller...?
along the street walking with her girlfriend, and you think to
yourself,
     lil girlfriend....why couldn't you just wait?
Do you see that 15-year-old sitting at the bus stop...
alone...
when she is seven months pregnant?
How about I see that 16-year-old girl with her mother at the
abortion clinic, and there are all sorts of picketers and shit out
front!
I feel their...pain,
but I said,
     no...no, not today, not today!

My mother...so strong...so beautiful...
Yet
I see her first with that scarf tied around her head...
I see her with little tread,
but no...wait...I now see her with one, not two, oh how I feel so
very...very blue!
     That's my moms!
She's there and I'm here
     How can I console her?
I feel I need to be near...her...to hold her, to tell her...I love her
I don't know how it feels to have one breast and not two, I don't
know how it feels to be cut...anywhere...especially...there!

This is the day!

I can't control them any longer
They are so warm and therapeutic,
I'm glad these tears are coming down my face…
today at a very steady pace
These tears have no fears,
no worries no doubts
I am happy they are here, so that I can move on to bigger and
better years.
These are My TEARS,
that is!

For My Daddy
*My father asked me to read one of my poems to him while he was in
my presence. I never got around to it. I guess I was too busy…or
something. So, I am writing one for him in hopes that it will make
him happy.*

My daddy is surely one of a kind, a man who would whoop
anyone's behind if needed. A man of limited words, but full
of kinesics, body language. Be careful not to piss him off,
he'll call you a cock sucka for sure!

Growing up, many friends of mine were afraid of him, especially when dating time came. His demeanor was that
of a man not to be messed with, you understand!

But my daddy has a big heart and most often he's misun-
derstood by his peers, family, children and friends. A heart
that has known many failures, fears, triumphs and victor-
ies.

When I was a child, he struggled to keep a 9-5, which
caused many issues in our home. Now looking back, he not
only had a craft, but was a marketer, an upholsterer, by and
large an entrepreneur with many circumstances.

My daddy, looking back, I can say he tried his best to be self
employed, not tied down by the white man's hand, as he
would say. My daddy is a great father, one who I respect,
value and honor.

My daddy, "Big Peach" my daddy. With love, your baby girl.

Lately, he speaks about leaving this place and it often bothers me, but it'll be ok. My father has seen many things, done many things, failed at many things, but he raised his children and was the best man and father he knew how to be.

New
I'm embarking on a new, a new that you may not be fond of, nor supportive of, but a new that I am not seeking your approval of.

This new has enhanced my being, almost like the feeling I got when I gave my life to Christ, His love showing itself here on earth through a new.

Oh yes, I'm embarking on a new, a new phase in my life, a new direction and dimension that I've never known, God is strengthening my faith and trust in Him through this new.

I don't expect you to understand, your opinions are your own, I take them like a grain of salt, but still, when fear, anxiety, jealously try to peak their ugly heads, I reach back and put my focus on Him because I know He has bought me the new.

Who Woulda Thought...?
Neva, in a million years, would I have thought I would end up here.
Pregnant without the child's father here by my side.
Once again, shattered dreams and broken promises, nails in a coffin...or so I thought.

But here I am, blessed to create a new life, begin a new life, live a new life, far from being dead, far from being over. With all that God promises still at my feet.
Everything happens for a reason, no weapon formed against me shall prosper...

Time and time again, your faith is tested, muzzling that selfish man, that humanity gets harder and harder daily...it does. Look

at where you are, what you've become, look at where you came
from and how much further you can and will go.
I will not let my anger consume me, although I want to rage an
all out war against him, with many attacks on his pride and ego,
but no, won't do any good.

I have to forgive and move on, knowing God is my rock, I shall not
be moved, and trouble on every side, but none will come near me.

But, who would have thought this was gonna be me, carrying
child number two and far from married.

Bills past due, but I got a fresh hair do, car note late, but I got
some new mix tapes... I tell you, what am I doing...?

Think and do, say and do, don't just sit... Think things through
and act upon the things that you are not attending to.

Oh, my feelings are hurt...my pride, I must set aside, get control
of my emotions and get with God on the inside.

The dude was taking me through ups and downs. I wanted him
to leave me alone, or so I thought, or simply wanted him to get it
together and make his word his bond and be the man he claimed
to be.

Who woulda thought, I would have ended up here, like so many
others who put their trust in man and took their eyes off God.

Goodbye Boop
I have let you go so many times and went right back to you.

This time was so different from all the others because I
now realize you were really a wolf in sheep's clothing.

When we met, you played on my weaknesses, knowing
you had no intention of fulfilling any dreams with me.

I said goodbye this time without saying goodbye. I truly
realize my self worth and now know that I have to love myself
more than any man could outside of God.

You see, I kept saying goodbye and at the same time I was
still saying hello; wanting you to provide me with the security
you knew you couldn't provide.

I love you, but I now love myself more.

You don't see my value, my mind, my worth. You have all of what you want and what you need, and I couldn't understand for the life of me why you still felt the need to be with me to steal love from me.

You left me empty inside, sad, lonely, clouding my mind with smoke and impurities, pitting me against myself. I admire the man you are, the strength you have for your family, but what about mine?

You left a bitter/sweet taste in my mouth so often that most nights I felt like lying in a coffin. But, I have a beautiful daughter and for her to continue to blossom, I must continue to blossom and not wilt on the inside.

So this time, goodbye is forever, without stating it, but simply stating, I can no longer be your mistress because it has brought me no life, but total stress and strife on the inside.

Goodbye Boop!!! And thank you for a life lesson well taught.

I have struggled with giving myself to others before getting to know them. I have a huge heart and I am a hopeless romantic, but as I grow, I am learning my true value and my value does not lie between my legs. I think we must esteem ourselves more and stop looking for happiness in other human beings and things. Someone told me that I find comfort in the undeserving, and at times I feel that there is truth in that statement, simply because I found myself repeatedly in situations that were not healthy for me. So now, I can say, I am giving to me, of me, loving me, and don't need to seek it elsewhere. So I know I will attract my king one day soon.

When I Wake

When I wake, you are there; my vision is clear, my path straight, and my heart at a steady pace.

When I am still, your presence lingers, thoughts of your caress sustain me when you are not near, your scent still lingering in the air.

When I work, I know that I work for us, assisting in the care of our family and future, helping to create sustainability...security.

When I sweat, I have no regret because I am keeping fit and healthy, exercising my mind and body to stay sharp and on point.

When I lay, your body helps me to feel secure, secure in knowing that you are here for me in more ways than I ever dreamed of, breathing for me when I feel I can't, knowing that you are mine, and were made just for me.

You have me, lock, stock and barrel, I'm not changing channels, I am here ready to build and grow with you, I hope you are up for the challenge and in it to win it.

Speak things into existence...let's spend some intimate time with God and acknowledge Him in all we do, let's speak blessings into our lives as He continues to bless us and our families.

When I am loving you, I am loving me, loving Him, loving being free from my past and insecure thoughts, loving that our family is beautiful and will not part.

Love you and pray, vow, hope, to never disappoint you nor lose any part of you in any way.

Breathe Love
It's amazing something so peaceful and surreal can walk into your life so unexpectedly and you flow with it like a crisp spring breeze

It's amazing how you have no worries or fears and everything around you and within you simply tells you to breathe

It was not like a whirlwind, there was no confusion

I was brought to shore, I'm sure

It wasn't all physical, it wasn't sexual at all

It was so spiritual and mental my ancestors begin to sing

inside of me, Breathe Love

The Other Day

> I read something the other day that made
> me wonder.... if I'm truly over you.

> I heard a song the other day that made me
> realize just how lonely I was with you, and
> just how lonely I am without you.

> I heard our daughter say something the other day that
> made me say, "oh, that's really her daddy in her."

> I saw something the other day that made me realize just
> how being apart has given us both an opportunity to
> receive from others what we could never give each other.

> I love you; I'm happy for you and I realized
> this the other day.

NATURE

I am staring out my window, watching time pass me by

I love to see the cardinal perched on top of the dog's cage

I see that rabbit that he would also love to chase

The wind is blowing across the fig tree

I also see the tall maple tree

The wind is blowing so peacefully and now I go

onto the porch to feel her sweet embrace

The sky is filled with huge cumulous clouds and I

close my eyes as the sun warms my face and I imagine

that I am asleep up there on a big fluffy pillow

I can smell the grass and I can hear the insects

These things we take for granted are the most

pleasant and loving in all the world, besides

A loving family especially enriched by little boys and girls

Matters of Your Heart

Have you ever awakened one morning and said to yourself, "I can't do this anymore"?
When you awake, you finally realized there is only one person in the world that has your best interest at heart.

When you realized you have to give yourself unconditional love.
When you realized how you have treated yourself like the shit on the bottom of your soles.

When you realized that it's finally time to move on and truly begin loving, embracing, smiling, laughing, breathing, and living for yourself.

When you realized that the relationship you were in didn't give you any substance, any love, any peace of mind.

When you realized that you were still lonely, unhappy, and for the first time complacent.

When you realized you had become totally dependent on another and still couldn't and will never give you all you need.

When you realized how selfish, self centered and narrow minded you had become.

When you realized how you abandoned all the individuals in your life, especially yourself.

When you realized you no longer knew who you were, or where this new person you've become came from.

When you realized you adopted someone else's false hopes, hoop dreams, money is everything, true love doesn't exist, false sense of reality.

When every thing you ever believed was bottled up, tucked away deep inside of you, and you awoke looking for it.

When you find any reason, any white lie, any piece of something that is nothing to try to help you change your heart, which is pretty made up, just like that bed you are so used to lying in.

When you finally realize there is nothing to really keep you, but all the things in the world to help you walk away.

When you realize something has always been nothing.

When it lacks unconditional love, when it lacks truth and honesty, when it lacks respect, honor, and joy.

No matter the matters of your heart, we will weather the storm.

What Should I Do?
My heart has been beating so fast

Because I know you won't be my last

I think about you everyday, and say to myself

"One day he will go away"

I am very fond of you in the most passionate way

But my feelings have yet to be seen

Because I'm feining for my friend at home yet I still yearn for you

and wonder what could actually be

But curiosity killed the cat, and my emotions couldn't handle

that

So I say to you, tell me what you want, and if it's meant to be then

our hearts will never stop

Moussa Ndiaye
I think he's pretty fly, smooth, cool, has me feelin his groove...has me on some kinda high...like butterflies in the sky...like we're dancing with tons of rhythm and we seem to be in tune.

Spirits and souls connecting, truly refreshing...to be in the presence of Moussa Ndiaye.

Tall, dark, lean and clean in body and mind...searching to see if our souls will intersect and become intertwined.

Each day I awake, wanting to know more about the country, mind and state, language and culture, something that I can take...apply to my life, creating a bind...

Of words, languages, cultures in the sublime

Moussa Ndiaye...Moussa Ndiaye...

Bonjour...Diama Ngma...Hello

Comment vas-tu?...Naga def?...How are you?

Je suis perdu (e)...Damaréere...I'm lost...
in you ...¡ y tu!

Merci...Dieuredieuf...Thank you!

Time...time...time...will only tell...
 Moussa Ndiaye
This poem includes French, Spanish and Wolof (native language of Senegal).

DEEP

Deep inside me there are many things I keep, many things that have seeped, like the disgusting juices piled up and compressed of the neighborhood trash, into loves of mine. Deep in the wholeness of my incompleteness, there resides an honesty that I'm afraid of, memories that terrify and lose me completely. Deep within is a love that springs forth with utterances of peace, serenity, confidence and joy...healing. Deep are the bruises, scars, soul ties that still leave scorn. Deep is my anger for those who lack patience and understanding, searching for answers to that which may be unexplainable, memories that are not trusting, loving or with reason nor clarity. Deep is a pride, a mother, a third generation of strength, education and dreams on high. Deep is my passion to live out my full potential that is as wide as all of the world's oceans and runs as long as the Nile. Deep is my love, my deepness I wanna share with you... in time, so hold on, move slow and we will stay afloat and not be lost or consumed by my deep...thoughts.

Thinking

I'm sitting, listening to the sounds around me

Sitting still and peaceful like an owl watching out for his night's prey

Sitting still, thinking, of all my wants and wishes, some of which I thought I had let slip away

The quiet, the peace, its music to my ears...almost virgin as I used to fear the total peace and quiet of my innermost thoughts

Connecting with my soul and binding up all negative thoughts

Some of which were hidden fears, silent cries and tears

Others of conquer, conquest and making a difference in another's life

Closing my eyes, breathing deep, with every inhale speaking "Be still" and with every exhale "Know that I am God"

There are so many wonders, so many treasures hidden in a day, just take a moment to be still, listen, and enjoy the night turning into day

Read to an elder that has lost his sight, have a conversation with a mother who's 93 and gain some insight

Help a kid with homework whose parents are overworked and underpaid, who's not home in time to play mother/father and maid

Take clothes to the women's shelter and share a word of conquering and overcoming a situation that has a young lady dismayed

Sit still, hear your thoughts and dreams and bring them into fruition with full pride and self-esteem

What's most rewarding about sitting still is the fact that you have tomorrow to do it all again

Probing
Where are my words?
Are they lost in my soul or bound up in many different worlds
The worlds of my forefathers, my ancestors...Bound up in time that has passed
My childhood, my youth...the pain of so many untold truths
Where are my words?
Are they written on my heart, stuck and implanted in my unspoken thoughts
Lost in the treasures of my forgotten, tossed to the side unclaimed high school treasures, that no one cared to measure the importance of
Where are my words?
Are they left behind with the anger of my unapologetic mother... my confused twisted older brother or with the sons of mothers who dehumanized a perfect little sister soldier
Where are my words?
Are they hiding in my pain, covering up what should have not been my shame, unexplained to those who inflicted the pain

Where are my words?
Are they with my Heavenly Father during my prayers, during my conversations said boldly with confirmation, affirming that I am healed, bold, courageous, prosperous and worth more than 24 karat gold...more than all the rubies and unclaimed stones of this earth
I ask, where are my words?
Are they with my new lover, my friendships of my true blue die hard sisters, my daughter who I try to keep in line and in order, or my father who has always been a father, but not always the best provider.
Where are my words?
Are they with the geese whom just took flight, the dogs who are strays, surviving with all their might, my people, places and things who are lost and without sight
Where are my words...where are my words? I ask again, where are my words?
Are they out in the air on a cold brisk winters night, speaking to my homeless brothers and sisters of the night, the pimps, prostitutes, alcoholics, drug dealers and drug abusers, running from those elusive demons...
Are they with my single unwed mothers, my brothers locked up for one reason or another, my people who have lost their fathers or mothers and other loved ones, my youth who have lost their direction and guidance, missing the opportunity to truly experience what it is like to be cool and not act like uneducated fools
Are they wrapped up in wisdom waiting to spring forth and become a force, make a difference in this world...sitting with my grandmother and elders who helped build this nation
Where are my words?

I Love 'em, I Do
I love the size of his hands, the span of his arms
I love how I dance in the twinkle of his eyes
I love his shoulders, the dimples in his cheeks, I especially love his beautiful brown eyes that captivate me when he speaks
I love the fact that he chose me, came back to me, to reside inside me and build a home and life with me, to raise our children and

be a family
I love his freshly shaven head and face,
I love the way he kisses my forehead, nose and cheek
I love 'em, I really do and I will not talk myself outta loving him, deeply, whole, completely
I even love the way we disagree, especially since he has a way of bringing 'me' back to 'me', not becoming stubborn and simply allowing my anger to get the best of me
I love the patience he exhibits with me, patience with my anger, my stubbornness, my spoiled ways, my show, or lack thereof, of intimacy
I love 'em, I really do, I love the way he prays with me, for me, over me, sharing his revelations of scripture with me
I Love 'em, I do

Postulating

I guess it's time that I really stop trying, this dating thing that is
I guess it's time for me to really give God a chance
Give myself some time for some true healing
See, I've never really been without a man, or some imitation of someone that resembled something like a man
I guess its time for me to dig deep within
Give my mind some peace and true relaxation, accomplish some things that have been plaguing me
So, it's time to tuck my heart away, hide it from those clones who may be lurking around night and day...
Time to let my soul fly free, become truly excited about being in the midst of me
Being happy with the woman God has fashioned of me
I guess I've given so much of myself to others, that I haven't given much of anything to me
So I guess in this season and spirit of giving, I'm giving my heart back to me and will prosper in the things that God has for me

When Is It Ok

When is it ok to fight
When is it ok to be angry
When is it ok to take flight

When is it ok to use all of your might

When is it ok to turn a deaf ear
When is it ok to show a little fear
When is it ok to suppress your feelings
When is it ok to seek some healing

When is it ok to keep your mouth shut
When is it ok to keep your mind shut

When is it ok to look the other way
When is it ok to say "It's ok"
When is it ok to have an opinion
When is it ok to live like you're in prison

When is it ok to hold and bite your tongue
When is it ok to go completely numb
When is it ok to admit you can't
When is it ok to admit you can't tackle all your problems
When is it ok to not want to solve them

When is it ok...

When is it ok to be alone
When is it ok to not be honored like you're the King on your throne and the Queen of your castle

When is it ok...

Broken Hearted
It's happened again
My heart bleeding through my pen
Yes, I've allowed myself to be hurt again
My guard wasn't completely down
And I slowly prepared myself for the bleakness I thought would turn around
But, I purposely left my heart open
Gave you a chance a second time
But this time you didn't have my mind
You didn't have me whole and completely because the trust you had to earn this go round

But the hurt I feel is for the way you've been absent in our daughter's life
You came in wit the line that you wanted to be wit her all the time
Yet 30 days have passed and you've only spent time with her one time, one evening
I close my eyes, shake my head and smile
My God is such an awesome God
The God you claim to know, but yet you struggle with being a father, a man to your children, but my excuse for you is, you simply don't know how, which shouldn't be an excuse at all
I'm so glad it's not me who took the fall
Nope, not this time, cause you have to own it, love it, live with it
And in due time, there will be no more hurt, cause my daughter has several fathers who won't cause her hurt

In closing, I sincerely hope, pray, wish that this work has inspired you, educated you, humored you and touched on every emotion imaginable, in hopes that you will grow from it and teach others what you know about life and what things to avoid. So I leave you with this:

I Wanna Be Free
I wanna be free
Free to dwell in the midst of me
Free to love in such a harsh society
Free to be in the presence of the bitter sweet

I wanna be free
Free to love in the midst of me
Free to be in a place and space where He resides
Free to allow my pain to subside

I wanna be free
Free to experience an oneness and peace with my soul
Free to be bold, courageous and solid gold
Free to allow my emotions to unfold

I wanna be free

Free to experience a first with another
Free to behold and uphold a certain quality and standard
Free to be unselfish and uncompromising

I wanna be free
I simply wanna be free to experience me

I am me
In my bare necessity
In my nakedness
In my flaws

In my period drawls.

I am me

In my imperfections
In my anger
In my hostility
In my everyday craziness.

I am me

In the midst of confusion
In the midst of loving
In the midst of destroying
In the midst of everything...

I am me...and greater is He that is within me!

Peace and blessings, beloveds.

Made in the USA
Columbia, SC
22 July 2020

14007452R00035